For David, who is all my Christmases —F.W.

For Violet and all her quacky relatives, here and everywhere —A.J.

Text copyright © 2017 by Frances Watts
Jacket art and interior illustrations copyright © 2017 by Ann James

All rights reserved. Published in the United States by Doubleday, an imprint of Random House Children's Books,
a division of Penguin Random House LLC, New York. Originally published in Australia by HarperCollins Children's Books,
a division of HarperCollins Publishers Australia Pty Limited, Sydney, in 2017.

Doubleday and the colophon are registered trademarks of Penguin Random House LLC.

Visit us on the Web! rhcbooks.com

Educators and librarians, for a variety of teaching tools, visit us at RHTeachersLibrarians.com

Library of Congress Cataloging-in-Publication Data is available upon request.
ISBN 978-0-593-17377-0 (trade) — ISBN 978-0-593-17378-7 (lib. bdg.) —
ISBN 978-0-593-17379-4 (ebook)

MANUFACTURED IN CHINA
10 9 8 7 6 5 4 3 2
First American Edition

A Very Quacky Christmas

by Frances Watts ★ illustrated by Ann James

DOUBLEDAY BOOKS FOR YOUNG READERS

amantha Duck was getting ready for Christmas.

We wish you a quacky Christmas, she sang
as she wound tinsel around the reeds.

"What are you doing, Samantha?"
asked her friend Sebastian.
"Animals don't put up Christmas decorations."

"We don't?"

"No," said Sebastian.
"Christmas is not for animals."

The next day, Sebastian found
Samantha hanging ornaments on a branch.
And that wasn't all. . . .

"What is that, Samantha?" Sebastian asked.

"It's my Christmas stocking."

Sebastian shook his head.
"I told you," he said.
"Christmas is not for animals."

When Sebastian visited Samantha the following afternoon,
she was writing on a long piece of paper.

We wish you a quacky Christmas, she sang.

"What are you doing now?" asked Sebastian.

"I'm making a Christmas list," his friend explained.
"I'm going to give presents to animals
all over the world!"

"What? That's impossible!" Sebastian said.
"Listen to me, Samantha:
Christmas is *not* for animals."

"Christmas is about giving and sharing, isn't it?" said Samantha.

"It is," Sebastian agreed.

"And animals like to give and share, don't they?"

"They do," said Sebastian.

"So, will you help me?" asked Samantha.

Sebastian sighed. "Of course."

"We'll make all the presents ourselves," Samantha decided.

"Make them all ourselves?" said Sebastian.
"Nonsense! It can't be done."

"Oh, yes, it can!" his friend replied.
"And we'll ask the other animals on the farm to help."

Samantha and Sebastian went to the sheep first.

"Christmas for animals?
What a wonderful idea!" said the sheep.
"We'll give you our wool."

All that day, and late into the night,
Samantha and Sebastian
knitted the wool into socks with spots
and scarves with stripes
and hats with pom-poms on top.

We wish you a quacky Christmas,
Samantha sang as their needles clicked.

The two friends went to the hens next.

"It's about time animals celebrated Christmas," said the hens.
"We'll give you our eggs."

All that day, and late into the night,
Samantha and Sebastian used the eggs to bake cupcakes.

We wish you a quacky Christmas, Samantha sang
as they iced the cupcakes in red and green.

They went to the cows last.

"Giving is what animals do best," said the cows.
"We'll give you the daisies in our field."

All that day, and late into the night,
Samantha and Sebastian wove
the flowers into daisy chains.

We wish you a quacky Christmas,
Samantha sang as they worked.

Then they wrapped the hats and socks
and scarves in brightly colored paper,
put the cupcakes in crackly cellophane,
and tied silver ribbon around the daisy chains.

By the time they were done, it was Christmas Eve.

"Now we have to deliver all these presents," said Samantha.

"Preposterous!" spluttered Sebastian.
"There is no way we can do it."

"Oh, yes, there is," his friend insisted.
"We'll ask the donkey to lend us his cart."

Samantha and Sebastian found
the donkey in the stables.

"Christmas is about sharing,"
said the donkey.
"I would be happy to
share my cart with you."

The two friends filled the cart with presents.

"We'll take a big run," said Samantha,
"and I'll flap my wings, and then we'll fly."

"An absurd idea," said Sebastian. "It'll never work."
But he helped his friend pull the cart
to one end of the biggest field.

Sebastian ran, and
Samantha flapped.
The cart full of presents
bumped and clattered
and rattled and swayed.
But it did not fly.

"Maybe I didn't flap hard enough,"
said Samantha. "Let's try again."

"This really is ridiculous," Sebastian thought
as they turned the cart around.

Sebastian ran across the field as fast as he could,
and Samantha flapped and flapped.
The cart full of presents jiggled and joggled
and jounced and bounced.
But it still didn't fly.

"You were right all along," said Samantha sadly.
"It *was* impossible. Maybe Christmas is not for animals."

Sebastian looked at the cart full of presents.

He thought of the sheep who had given their wool,
the hens who had given their eggs,
and the cows who had given their daisies.

He thought of the donkey who had lent his cart.

And he thought of Samantha, who had worked so hard
to share Christmas with animals all over the world.

"No," Sebastian said slowly. "*You* were right all along.
Christmas *is* for animals. Let's try one last time."

So they turned the cart around one last time, and
one last time they ran and flapped across the field.

And as the evening star rose into the dusky sky,
Sebastian and Samantha and the cart full of presents rose too.

"We did it!" said Samantha. "We're flying!"

They rose higher and higher, till the farm was just a tiny dot below.

Samantha gave a loud, happy quack, then began to sing:

We wish you a quacky Christmas.
We wish you a quacky Christmas. . . .

On Christmas morning,
animals all over the world
woke up to find a special surprise.

The farm was blanketed in sunshine when Samantha and Sebastian arrived home with their empty cart.

Or was it empty?

Not quite . . .

While Samantha and Sebastian opened their presents,
they both sang Samantha's favorite Christmas song.

We wish you a quacky Christmas.
We wish you a quacky Christmas.
We wish you a quacky Christmas . . .

And a ducky new year!